Marlot & Zed

Noah Walker

Published by Free Spirit

www.freespiritpublisher.com

First Edition February 2023

Cover Design by Koni Deeraz, Germany

Cover Concept Design by Brandon Williams, USA

Book Design by Adil Ilyas, Pakistan

Edited By Tonya Walker - United States

KZ Razavi, India

ISBN: 978-93-95193-60-3

Price: $15 USD

BCID: 651-16791403

On their walk back they talked about normal things. About Charlotte.

"Yeah…" Zed's frown locked under the harbour lights. She elected to end things in the morning, but she couldn't bring herself to say it. So, they watched the boats instead. A ferry floated between the cities and men in one-pieces wound down whatever it is men wind down at water treatment plants. A faint bleating retreated behind the warehouse doors.

And it was Marlot's turn to frown. And Zed stared at her feet. But the water… eventually they both just looked at the water.

*

The hospital is loud. Units pumping air burr sound, but he sits still. He watches his phone, and it buzzes.

At least she's not alone. In fact, he's sat across from her for the last hour. Every now and again he walks over and studies her face, before sitting down and returning to his emails. They're not important emails, just automated messages: double-first-name kinds of men requesting money for the third district. Eventually there were no more emails. He waited a little while longer, but there was a knock at the door.

Marlot closed his phone.

"How are you doing?" the doctor asked. He shrugged and said he was okay. The doctor motioned that she'd be back in a moment. And the moment passed slow.

Eventually, Zed called. From their messages, it seemed her day was going well, but he didn't want to answer. He didn't want to talk on the phone next to Meredith in the hospital. He took a picture of her instead and thought of sending it to Zed, but of course the doctor returned; the hospital needed the room. Marlot said "I'm ready," and then, "thank you."

The doctor nodded a sharp, impatient nod and escorted him to the front. The loud space became louder as he moved toward the lobby.

"I'm not a betting man so, I won't..." and, "You have to begin to take responsibility..." among other statements, flew around. The air felt recycled like in an airport. He said, "God the air is dry," and the doctor frowned. Marlot had that effect.

Still, even he had someone to call upon exiting the hospital. Ms. Carter, or Elizabeth, or Zed, as she now called herself, would, on occasion, talk to the 23-year-old. She found Marlot interesting, if not young, and would laugh to her friends saying, "Never twice in a week." Her friends found this amusing.

Privately, Zed liked Marlot, but she was 25. She was a girl with a job at an office in an industry with a cubicle *papier mâchéd* in post-it notes. Post-it notes amused her. She worked in fashion and had worked in fashion since moving to the city.

Marlot worked in magazines. Or a magazine, for there was only one. But it didn't matter. He was rich by association. Meredith had purchased their apartment after her book blew up. *Living Large with Lung Cancer* was all about dealing with diagnosis, but it was also about sex after diagnosis which many people liked. She talked about coping mechanisms and CBD gummies and family, which Marlot found ironic. He was told it was very inspirational.

But then she died, so how inspirational is that? That's what Marlot was thinking as he left the hospital. Still, he could not help but miss her. He missed her wit, and he missed what she'd say about the fans that approached her about her book. "They're really very sweet," she'd say, but she'd say that about just about anything. But what could she do, they loved her. And they asked her to speak in front of other people who had already read her book.

At the Hilton or the Marriot, or, eventually, the Barnes and Noble in the city, she'd speak about her book but mostly she'd answer questions. Men and women who knew dying people would attend, which, to Marlot's surprise, was just about everyone. Between the reading and the questions, Meredith would go out to smoke and fans would ask her why she smoked, and she would say she liked it.

It's bad for you, they'd say.

"I'm going to die either way…" she'd want to say, but you can't tell that to people whose loved ones are dying of cancer. So instead, she'd say she'd rather smoke, but this did little to comfort her observers.

Marlot loved this part of the story. He thought it was funny, and, it seemed, that Meredith also found it funny. When he went to join her, just to sit and chat between breaks, they'd share looks and smiles as different people expressed their versions of surprise and advice. The people who idolized his mother found it grating. Their frustration caused him to smile.

For this and other reasons, Meredith's fans did not like Marlot. He wondered what they expected. When asked what he wanted to do, Marlot said he'd like to be an author, a *real* author, a distinction people despise. Marlot said he didn't care.

Zed told Marlot that he should care. "I am already rich," he'd say. She'd shake her head with all the weight of her shoulders. Of course, this was the problem.

When Marlot called her back, he called from the sidewalk. Zed was working, but she liked when Marlot called so she answered between sips of coffee and a finger held to an intern.

She said, "Why hello, Marlot." in the way that people said, "Why hello," in older movies. Marlot replied, "My mother died," in a dramatic sort of way, but her death was not dramatic. Instead, she died typing, between breaks at their kitchen table. Zed was sad to hear she'd gone.

She told him she was sorry, and he felt that she felt sorry. She asked if he wanted to talk about it, but he refused. Instead, he asked for a drink, perhaps later, perhaps in her part of town.

She agreed to meet him somewhere or elsewhere whenever he was ready, and so he picked a time and said that he would see her there.

He took the train because his mother lived in Brooklyn. So did he and Zed. Although Zed liked the city, she wanted to leave. She could have talked about Los Angeles or San Diego if Marlot asked, but he wouldn't, hadn't and didn't. So, she just thought about it to herself. She told her friends and they nodded knowingly for their boyfriends talked only of themselves. Zed told herself that Marlot was different from their boyfriends because he was not quite as stupid. But he was also not her boyfriend, a thought she revisited as she hung up the phone.

*

At the office, her intern asked for time off, which Zed found funny. The interns at AVT were unpaid. Still, Zed nodded, and the intern smiled, and shuffled away to make the next four hours disappear. At AVT, interns existed in the same way that Zed's platforms existed: for effect.

For the company, interns represented investment opportunities, and for the interns, an assuagement of fears carried by the parents of artists. Of course, interning in fashion is far less art-filled than the payless employees might have imagined, but where else were they to go?

Even Zed struggled to retain the art in her job. These days, she spent most of her time developing software which she didn't inherently love. Still, there was more opportunity and she felt she deserved a better role than *Design Assistant,* so she began to develop AVT's new calendar.

Where Prada designed clothes, AVT existed to help brands like Prada design clothes. Each brand had their own release calendar and schedule which made it difficult for any one person to know what was going on for the whole company. Zed began learning how to consolidate all these calendars into a Master Calendar and was almost done with the Beta.

In learning the practice, she separated herself from the clothes she wanted to design. She could only pour herself so many places. How could there be time for art?

Hours later, she'd offer the question to Marlot. Although he wrote professionally, he did not feel much like an artist. Not now, anyway. The last year and a half hadn't really been about that. Instead, he told her about his phone calls.

His phone erupted for interviews that his desire for celebrity compelled him to take. The phrasing of the emails appeared to offer sympathy, but the nature of the questions suggested something more poisonous.

Still, he'd meet with *The Post* on Thursday. Zed refocused brought him back around to the question, and he frowned.

"I don't know," he finally said, rubbing his scalp in his hands. "Are you really entertaining multiple options? Like, are we really talking about you quitting?"

Zed reflected and supposed she was more trying to come to terms with the fact that her next move would be corporate. She felt discomfort in this realization, and resentment toward his relative availability. At twenty-one hours a week, no rent, and food paid, she found his position envious. And yet Marlot languished on his mother's laurels. She thought this over as she watched him play with the lip of his drink. He looked over at the bar.

Still, his eyes were puffy. The black vacuums with which he expressed himself also expressed emotion. He apologized and looked away. Zed smiled, "Let's go for a walk."

The suburbs were never quiet, but they were quieter than the city. Small celebrations covered the corners and every now and again, a small fireworks display lit up the sky. Marlot moved quietly awhile. The air was warm but refreshing and his eyes dried as they walked.

"You..." he began. "Thank you." Zed grabbed his hand and pulled him in a long arc until he faced her. Her breath smelled like alcohol. He swallowed as she looked up at him. He breathed through his nose. His heart felt like it was moving.

*

By Wednesday, he began to regret the *Post.* He thought of canceling when an offer to film the interview made the limelight brighter. Marlot prepared his makeup.

The morning of the shoot, he managed to sleep and wake at normal times. Although the interview would necessarily cover his mother, his inheritance of her capital would surely be accompanied with a question of what's next. At least, Marlot presumed their interest.

In striving to take the world in stride, he relaxed his grip on his personality and made a note to consider the therapy he might require to regain balance.

Lost mother aside, his increasingly sedentary lifestyle was having effects and summer, despite its light, equaled winter in the efforts he made to stay indoors. Regardless, he would get out today. The studio was on 57th. Marlot took the train.

*

The studio was underwhelming. In the place of modern fixtures and camera equipment, a couple chairs and a DSLR and a light angled down ten feet above the ground.

Jesus, he thought. It felt harsh and thrown together. Upon further inspection, Marlot found the *Post's* YouTube channel underwhelming. He wished he had not placed so much on so little. Regardless, minor celebrity beats aspiring celebrity, a thought he kept as he met the man who led with his hand.

My name's Jim, said Jim, and Jim said he would be the one conducting the interview today. Jim, as it turns out, was the *Post's* entertainment editor.

"A gay Republican, I know," he laughed, "it happens," and Marlot found this appealing. Still, he did not know how to respond. Jim carried on, and Marlot made conversation and asked Jim what he liked about his job. Jim said he liked the commentary and its influence on directors. Webber's show is getting a rewrite because of me, he bragged. He told Marlot about his nickname. "The Butcher of Broadway" offered Marlot a seat.

Marlot's forehead began beading, and he asked the potentially not-so-gentle man whether they had a makeup artist onsite. Jim said, no, but they had a bathroom. These two things were not the same and Jim looked particularly well groomed for a location without a makeup artist. The energy in the room seemed professional but Marlot felt he'd met a dangerous man. Laughing and smiling far more than Marlot generally allowed, he departed to the bathroom and tried to manage his anxiety. Best to not look stupid, he thought. He poured over his supplies.

Face dried, he picked up his stack of papers. He would sit down prepared if nothing else. Jim again offered him a seat and said he'd be along in a moment. The light was on by this point and sweat built underneath Marlot's makeup.

He stood to retreat from the light, but a stern look from the camera man put the 23-year-old back in his chair. An intern came by with water, and he thanked him for the hospitality. Jim returned and sat in a softer second light, giving Marlot reason to ask if they could turn down the canon bleaching his pores.

This awfully awkward joke hit the room with a pause, and a cough came back from the sound engineer. The answer, it seemed, was no.

Jim began the show. He ran through a list of entertainment news before introducing Marlot.

"Early Monday afternoon, acclaimed author and activist Meredith Marlot passed away at home. Sources report the best-selling author died in the midst of writing her unreleased manuscript, leaving many to wonder about its future."

Marlot twitched in his seat. In a moment, a bead of sweat would slide down his face. No one had mentioned the manuscript. *Just wondering what it's like to lose such an incredible woman,* they had said. And yet, "The content remains secret. Speaking to that end, ladies and gentlemen, her son, Michael Marlot."

An obvious silence followed. Marlot could hear it, but he smiled: Hey Jim, thank you for having me.

"So, Michael,"

"I prefer to go by Marlot," Marlot interrupted.

Jim's grin grimaced, before he returned to his smile, "Of course, naturally. Marlot, how are you doing?"

"Thank you for asking, Jim. I'm hanging in there. Naturally, the loss of a mother is hard for anyone to bear, but after my father's passing, I mean that was so long ago, well, it doesn't matter. I suppose I've felt alone these last few days."

Jim stared deep into Marlot's eyes. "I can only imagine. Were you and your mother close?"

"We had our ups and downs like any family," Marlot began, "but we loved each other. I don't know. We lived together. By the end, our relationship became professional."

"What do you mean?" Jim asked.

"I suppose I mean we treated each other as writers in residence with one another. She would pass along her writing, and I'd pass mine along to her, and together, we produced our products."

"Such as *Living Large with Lung Cancer…*"

"Yes, but she has written many things. Although that's what made her famous…"

"Well, you would know after all. You are also writer, correct?"

"Yes,"

"How has your work been going?"

"It's been going well. I think my work is treated unfairly. But this more recent piece I've been working has, I don't know, elements of truth to it. I believe in it at least. I brought…"

"That's fantastic! Generational genius, once you've published, of course." He winked. Marlot almost looked for the audience he referenced. "Were you able to read a little of her most recent work?"

Marlot bristled, "Yes."

In truth, she had not really worked on much after she struck the deal with her publisher. Her condition had her dead long before Monday. After a time, writing was not her priority.

The inevitable follow up followed.

"And?" Jim implored.

"And nothing, I suppose."

"Will it not be released?"

"I guess we'll see, it kind of depends." Marlot grasped for straws.

Jim did not seem pleased by this answer. "On what?" but Marlot just sat on the opposing end, silent.

Jim pivoted.

"Do you think your mother respected your work? Jim asked.

"Yes, at least I think she believed in me."

"Do you think that's why she decided to donate her estate?"

Marlot blinked. "Pardon me?"

"What will you do for work now that you can no longer work from home?"

*

Marlot left the interview flustered. Jim thanked him for coming and said he would send along a cut before publishing the video. He did not agree to make any edits in advance of the release, but such things can't be helped. Marlot was more immediately concerned with his financial situation. He called his mother's lawyer for confirmation.

"Hey Mackenzie, I just found out in an interview that I'm losing the estate. Is this misinformation or did you fail to notify me?"

"We were going to notify you today. The information leaked. I'm sorry Marlot."

"It's…" a siren wailed by. Marlot's heartbeat quickly now.

"Pardon?"

"It's alright!" Marlot screamed as the sirens dissipated. A couple passing looked back and Marlot waved apologetically and offered a sort of smile. The lady on the phone paused.

"I'm sure it's quite a shock."

Marlot laughed. "Yes, Mackenzie, it's quite a shock."

*

Zed digested the information. The fragile young man shifted on the other side of Face Time. The pervading "what now" of the situation loomed. Will the magazine give you more hours? Marlot laughed, dejected.

"It's not funny!"

"I know, I…" he swallowed, "My goodness I know."

Zed's face softened. "What are you making now?"

"Around $15,000"

"Christ, Marlot. You need a job."

"Are you hiring?" he laughed. And they sat in silence for a while. "Hey, I'm going to call you back."

The receiver clicked. Zed stared at her phone. She was not exactly in a place to offer jobs, and even if she were, she wondered about recommending Marlot. He was, at best, adequate.

"If you need help on WordPress," she could imagine him saying, but the world is much larger than WordPress. She decided to take lunch early.

*

Marlot's eyes were no longer ingesting. Stacks of responsibilities covered his mother's kitchen table. Approaching any or each of them appeared improbable. His mother's will gave him her possessions, but that amounted to a stack of books.

She wanted him to work despite her illness, and now he knew why. He wished he hadn't hung up on Zed, but he didn't know what to say. A walk, perhaps. Yeah, perhaps a walk would clear everything up.

Pushing back from the table, Marlot stood and dressed and raided his mother's medicine cabinet. Ever medicated, prescription and otherwise, he sifted through her allotted pain medication, but decided to settle on smoking.

Her less-than-medical prescription made him smile as he rolled three grams out his door and to the park. I need an assistant, he thought, but first he'd need a job. At least writers flourish in the city.

The magazine he worked for published climbing content out of an office in Toronto. He found the sport appealing because it did not ask you to do things in any particular way. Although there were coaches, Marlot had found the process best enjoyed alone. It was his primary decompressor.

Despite his attitude problem, Marlot got along with climbers. Nobody there talked about anything other than climbing and effort was prioritized over ability. Marlot often felt he expended a lot of effort. That said, being strong also appealed to Marlot, but only in a vague, masculine sort of way.

Although he was tall, and maybe somewhat mannish, he took efforts to soften his complexion. Maybe this was part of living near a city, but he identified with women more than men. He found men lacked depth. They seemed concerned about their identity. Women seemed more fluid, more capable of understanding the nuance of being a person.

Zed asked if he'd ever consider writing from the perspective of a woman, but he said he doubt he could. Meredith said a person feels when what they're saying's wrong, and that's how Marlot felt when he tried to write as a woman.

His brain fuzzed as he made his way uptown. These thoughts that he found profound, but were perhaps slides from Instagram, evaporated. By the time the sun had fallen, he'd made it to the gym. He breathed a little easier.

*

The morning's publication did not come with the transcription Jim had promised. Instead, *Meredith Marlot Strips Deadbeat Son of Inheritance*. The subhead followed softer, *She has donated her estate to equitable institutions.*

If Marlot had a publicist he might have crafted a response, but he did not. Instead, he sighed. After everything else, being called a *deadbeat* didn't really hurt. Maybe it hits harder when someone continues to support your lifestyle despite your inaction. Marlot was conscious of having lost his already, so he swallowed and made his coffee.

He showered as the water boiled. After, he called Zed, but Zed was busy. Shrugging, he searched for therapists in his area and set an appointment. He did not know whether his mother's insurance still covered him, but he figured they could only move so fast. With a meeting set for the next day, Marlot focused on planning his mother's funeral. Meredith's agent and her manager had taken many of the necessary steps and needed only his signature on the more sensitive documents.

His signing and resending felt burdensome today. The funeral would be Monday, two weeks before he'd have to move out. In finding a new place to stay, he had options geographically, but lacked options economically. A job, then. Perhaps a job would help.

*

Her intern had offered to grab it for her, but Gong Cha was sacred. Normally she walked down Boulevard, and thought about her line, or her designers, but today she thought about Calvin. He walked with her, quieter than she would have imagined.

Calvin kept almost saying something. He did not stutter, but instead chose openings that were specific before detracting into something vague or ambiguous. "I've been thinking of talking to Matilda," his manager, he'd begin, and then, losing his nerve would finish, "about her Greek salad recipe." Zed would look over at him skeptically and say something like "Yeah, it was pretty good. Can't believe it's been over a year since she brought it to the office."

Then she'd stare at his downturned head until he said something else stupid. Still, Zed quite liked Calvin. They started at AVT together out of college and spent the preceding four years leading their design class. They moved to the city together by chance, but it's less of a chance when your only other option is Los Angeles.

Despite his unique sense of style in school, Calvin was predictable. He and his partner had been all but married for the last six years and, if all went to plan, would be married within the next six.

Alien, Zed thought, but it was not her life to live. The condensation caused her fingers to slip a little on the Bubble Tea, but she caught it with a lurching motion.

Calvin looked up. "What?" Zed challenged. He giggled and opened his hands defensively.

"No retort?"

"No, I'm sorry." He tried to grin. It looked ghastly. Zed liked the word and told him that his grin looked ghastly. Once more he was on the defense. Zed looked at him with an expression she considered frank looking. Very matter of fact. "What has you so inside yourself?"

Calvin sipped contemplatively. "I think I need another job." To Zed, this did not strike her as a crisis, but allowing him his drama, she replied, "Why?"

"Bobby and I are thinking of getting a house."

Of course, they were, Zed thought. She had only met Bobby once or twice, but the couple very much reflected the family values inherent to the South. Calvin grew up in Virginia. Still, he was only 24. Zed asked what was wrong with the job, and he said it wasn't enough.

"$65,000 was great when I was living alone, but now with the house... I mean we can't stay in the city off sixty-five-grand," his frown furrowed into his brow.

Zed's brow deepened. She'd have to save it for later. Calvin looked at her from across the table and Zed tried to push past her own feelings. Her lip twitched. She clearly looked uncomfortable because Calvin grew concerned.

"What is it?" he asked. She was quiet.

He pushed back into his chair and stare around them. The square began filling with lunchers." Calvin smiled at a family walking a toddler around the fountain.

After a while, Zed watched them as well.

"Calvin, I make $45,000 a year."

Understanding, he blinked sympathetically. "Oh, Zed."

She teared up. Her mouth dropped and her hand collided with the table. Her Bubble Tea hopped and landed back on the surface. Diners looked over at the upset couple.

Michael reached out his hand.

"I'm learning software, Calvin. Fucking software, and they have the gall to pay me less than my fucking classmate?"

"Maybe it's a mistake," Calvin knew as he said it that he had missed an opportunity to offer a different response. Zed looked at him dejected and Michael changed tact. "Maybe you and I can go talk to them."

Zed's frown softened and she sighed, "You are very sweet, Calvin." She would always say that when she discounted another's assistance, "It's quite alright, thank you. I'm sorry."

Calvin exhaled and rubbed his hands together anxiously, "Yeah, of course, no worries."

The sun blared down from above and baked them into the concrete. Zed wondered why she'd moved to the city.

*

Despite all he'd built it up to being, the office was much like any doctor's: patients filled the chairs by his side. Of course, a therapist is not a doctor and so Marlot wondered what exactly they were qualified for, but then again, it didn't really matter. The lady at the desk offered him a lollipop. He borrowed her pen. It had a plastic flower glued to the end.

Marlot wrote his last name first and then scratched it out. He printed Michael Marlot into the boxes at the top of the sheet. He wondered what the lady would think.

Another lady came in through the side door and called a name. A man stood and walked out of the door. There were more people here than he'd anticipated, more children.

A girl in her teens typed next to her mother as her mother scrolled on a phone. Marlot watched the pair until he realized his staring. The girl's typing increased in rapidity. The apple keys clattered and Marlot tried to read his book. Stevie Nicks played over the ceiling's speakers.

His mind sang the lyrics over the words he read, and often that meant rereading the page.

"Anderson. Anna Louise, Anderson," called a stocky man from the door.

Marlot joined the daughter in looking up. Her mother stood clutching her phone to her chest. She looked back at her daughter. The girl reached up and squeezed her mother's hand. Anna Louise Anderson slipped her phone into her purse and smiled at the massive nurse. Her ring made a sound as she gripped the door handle. The younger Anderson watched Anna Louise before turning her head back to her typing.

As the younger Anderson typed, different people made their way to the back rooms. They all looked different from Marlot. He wondered if 23-year-olds came later in the day. Marlot knew many people who never went to therapy. Were they more mentally sound?

The stocky assistant returned. He said his name and Marlot looked sharply at the man and then around the room. "Yes?"

"We're ready for you."

Marlot stood and the girl looked at him and he looked back at the girl. Some blank sympathy or fear or shame or pride shot between them. Or maybe he imagined it. Maybe he shouldn't have made eye contact at all. Maybe it was good he'd gone to therapy.

*

As it turned out Zed was right. What had begun as the $45,000 on-boarding salary had grown, for Calvin, into the sixty-five grand he now made.

Calvin spoke of legal retribution, but Zed hoped to retain her job and make back her money.

"It's illegal, plain and simple," Calvin said between sips of his iced latte.

"I don't know if it's illegal, but it's ugly."

"Do you think you'll go public?" She watched him relish the story's potential. He looked over from her side.

"I don't think that will be necessary," she said.

"At least you have money coming your way,"

Zed hoped so. Although she felt herself to have good grounds, her boss, a gold-spectacled Mr. Mooney, was everything before empathetic.

They'd spoken twice, and only on one occasion did he engage. When Mr. Mooney hired her and Calvin, they, along with all new hires at AVT, were subjected to a screening. He asked them a question or two about themselves and then set his expectations.

"If all goes well, we'll never speak," he'd said. Then he tilted his glasses down the bridge of his nose. "Is that understood?" Zed had gulped, nodded, and thanked Mr. Mooney for the opportunity.

Two years later, she did not feel the same reverence for the balding fashion designer. He inspired fear, but in the sort of way that affects people without leverage the most. The social landscape was changing, and Mooney would have to recognize it. A person does not get to pay their workers whatever those workers will accept. No. There are standards, Zed thought. There are standards.

Zed carried these words from coffee across Boulevard, and up the elevator. I could put it in an email she thought, but it felt inexpressive. Now that she stood on the precipice, however... Now that she looked at Mooney and his glasses and his glass walls and clean desk, and bullet proof expression...

He looked up from his desk. Her heart hiccupped. Her knuckles wrapped the door. Silence followed. She felt even the printer paused in surprise. Mooney did not have meetings in his office. Mooney ensured this by removing the colours and chairs that might welcome a normal person. His door is even locked to ensure separability.

The steps still made sounds through his carpet. His creaseless Silvano Lattanzi's pierced the door's fogging glass. The latch slid into a crisp "click." Zed stood in the centre. Her hands crossed defensively. The man in clean lines stood before her. He had taken off his glasses.

*

She held her ground. At some point Marlot had begun what he called "talking in a loud voice." Clawson appeared unperturbed as he yelled about the *Post.* Clawson nodded vaguely and wiped her glasses, indifferent. Marlot began talking about her as well. His increasingly antagonizing perspective stripped Marlot of his compromised credibility. At some point he was standing, ranting into the room's corners. He looked back at her and spat.

"You're just like my mother."

Clawson raised an eyebrow. Marlot sat down and they listened to the silence awhile.

Marlot's anger subsided leaving him with a woman who bore Marlot's "increased volume" for the better part of an hour. His face started to redden, and he returned to the same hands he stared at in the waiting room. Her eyes pierced his lids through his downcast gaze. He shivered and looked up.

But she just looked on, waiting from behind her wide-framed glasses. In fact, these were much like his mother's.

Despite what he had said, Clawson differed from Meredith. Instead, she looked upon him contemplatively. There was no retort. No, "and," or, "You done?" for him to awkwardly contend with. Instead, she asked, "How are you feeling?"

They agreed to meet again on Wednesday. Marlot felt ashamed for asking anything after the session they'd had, but his tears dried, and he felt lighter. It felt good to talk. Sometimes he felt he used Zed ruthlessly: a sounding board made flappable by days of noise. He would have to thank her. He'd have to thank Clawson as well.

When he spilled onto the street, it was humid. He called Zed, but the call went to her voicemail. He sighed and tried to figure out the time by staring at the clouds. When he couldn't, he looked to the ground and started walking.

*

Zed went home. She grabbed her bag and binder and pencils and phone. Then she left. Calvin looked at her from the side, but Zed stared obstinately at the floor. "Fucking humiliating," she muttered, and Calvin looked at Matilda who had more or less spent the last three minutes aghast.

"I'll be right back."

Matilda nodded absently. The office rang with a dull silence. Zed's interns wiped down her desk. They would talk in the back room later. Mooney's office door closed with a click. Zed played it over in her head.

"For Calvin, we had expectations."

The carpet disappeared in front of her. It turned into the tiled floors of the elevator. Then the lobby. Then a pair of shoes. It was Calvin. His eyes had become so big. The water on his eyes seemed to magnify them. Zed felt dark.

"Cal, I don't…"

He hugged her, and then he hugged her tighter. Her temple pressed against his clavicle. He kissed her head. "Call me if you need me," he said.

Zed nodded, "Thanks." The air stuck to her throat.

*

Her phone rang but she was painting. She let it ring on the nightstand, by her bed, in the room she was not sitting. She sat in the kitchen. Her floor was covered with newspapers that caught the falling paint.

Zed watched it fall. She scooped little dollops out of Behr buckets with a spoon. When they splattered on the canvas, she'd smile. Plop, plop, plop, she said. And the paints continued plopping. When it was covered, she put it on an easel and watched it dry. It was not anything. Just action.

Zed stood to grab her phone. The call from earlier was Marlot and she called him back.

"Hey," she said.

"Hey," he replied.

"What?"

"What? Nothing. What?" Zed fell silent. Marlot was also silent. "I, uhh. I went to therapy."

Zed blinked. She turned on Face Time. It was Marlot's turn to blink. "Hey," he said.

"How was it?" Zed watched him through her phone. He reddened and looked all about him.

"It was good. I uhm… What are you up to?"

"Nothing," she paused. "Ugh, nothing it's fine. Why?" Zed was groaning.

Marlot vibrated. "Have you had dinner?"

Zed hadn't had anything since the bubble tea. Marlot braced himself, "I wanted to thank you. I don't know if you are around or available but if I could buy you dinner… I'm already in your neighbourhood if you want to eat."

Zed came out of herself and looked at the boy through cell phone. He set is face so seriously, and Zed laughed in spite of herself.

"What?" Marlot offered, and Zed just laughed more. "You're already in my neighborhood?" She smiled. "I'd love to, I'll be down in a sec."

*

At dinner Marlot expressed emotions. Zed found his efforts to approach vulnerability amusing but, in the end, she was happy he'd come all the way to see her. "Marlot," Zed said, "I do not need you to be anyone other than who you want to be." Marlot said thank you but looked down below the lip of their table.

She reached a hand across the table. She touched his forearm, "But thank you. It means a lot." Marlot smiled. His eyes looked up at her. She looked back at his face. His eyes deepened, and she said, "What?" as he said "Nothing, nothing," Marlot grinned. They finished their entrees.

As promised Marlot grabbed the bill and asked Zed if she'd ever been by the water. It's so close, he said, and she noted that it was close.

Feeling smooth after their dinner's wine, she put her arm through his elbow, and they walked into the breeze. The day's heaviness blew on the wind and made its effects less potent. They bought tall boys at the deli.

*

The sun had all but gone by the time they hit the east river, and while she'd seen it before, it was made special by Marlot's wanting to show her. The sun stripped between the buildings on the island. The water, despite its murkiness, reflected the hotter oranges of the escaping light. Zed sat quietly awhile. Marlot fidgeted with his fingers and affected some sort of relaxed pose on the cement wall they rested on.

*

The wind picked up further. The smell of the East River was replaced with the smell of rain. "It's not supposed to rain," he said. Zed looked at him. The fading light illuminated the right side of her face. He told her so and then felt very silly. What is it that people talk about? Normally he'd just talk until they parted.

"How was your day?"

Zed looked over at him. Was his face reddening or was it just the light? Zed sighed. She guessed that it was actually pretty good. "It was okay, I got a raise."

Marlot raised an eyebrow, "Wow, congratulations."

It was Zed's turn to sigh, but it didn't feel so traumatic talking to Marlot. She told him about Mooney and about Calvin.

"$20,000 difference," Marlot whistled.

"They won't reimburse me for the time I should have been getting paid the sixty-five."

"Damn, so that's, what, a cumulative forty-ish you've missed out on?"

Zed nodded.

"Have you talked to the other women at your company?"

She shook her head, "I left afterward. You should have been there Marlot. This guy, this fucking guy just stared at me. I don't think I yelled, but everyone in the office was listening." She started to grin by the end of her sentence.

Marlot laughed suddenly

"What?" Zed grinned,

Marlot smiled "Did it feel good?"

"Yeah. It did." Her smile was wide now, but then it started fading. She said it started feeling bad after a while though. "I just feel like I stumbled onto a truth I already knew. I felt it wouldn't happen to me. It's fashion, you know, I just thought…"

"It would be fair?"

"Yeah, that it would be fair and easy and it's not and I hate it! I hate feeling duped by the people who hired me. I hate that I am working harder for less. I hate that this stunt today will still affect my future hiring prospects even though I was entirely in the right. I love being me, but sometimes…"

The wind came on faster now. Zed stared at her acrylics and Marlot stared at Zed's acrylics. "It's not fair," Marlot began, and Zed barked a laugh, cutting him off. She felt bad about it as he returned his gaze to his own hands, "Obviously it's not fair, but I bet you made more allies than you lost today."

Zed looked at Marlot. A thin drop splashed on her arm. "Will it always be this way?" Marlot looked back at her. "I don't know." The rain began to fall.

*

Mourners sent flowers on the weekend. Most ended up with her agent, but some found his address. The cards that accompanied said "You will be missed," and, "Thank you," and Marlot watched them accumulate behind the doors beside his living room.

By Sunday, he had amassed so many that he began building a place for them outside. Passersby would pick flowers from his baskets, and he'd watch them in his time away from work.

On Monday he collected the notes and placed them in a shoe box he'd bring to the funeral. He and his agent decided on a private occasion. "We could go public," her agent suggested, "but they agreed that a live stream of the service would suit whoever wished to watch the proceedings.

Marlot buttoned his buttons. He tied his tie and stared into the mirror of his mother's bathroom. Her jars and bottles and candles still sat in the same ring stains leftover by excess product. Her brush still had hair on it.

He picked it up but put it to the side. His hair had decided to go all of the directions, but he left it as it was. His mother would have told him to get it cut. Marlot threw his jacket over his shoulders.

At 12:15, Zed met Marlot at his door. "I'm here," she said into the microphone, and Marlot buzzed her in.

"Don't you look nice," Zed affected, and Marlot flushed remembering their moment in the rain.

"You look nice too."

Zed did a twirl. She looked about the apartment and commented on the "greenhouse," growing in his foyer. Marlot shook himself awake.

"She's literally dead. Who do they think they're thanking?"

Zed laughed and Marlot smiled, and the pair left the building. Marlot ordered a car and the Uber asked where they were going dressed so fancy on a Monday afternoon. "My mother's funeral," Marlot said flatly, and the driver quickly redacted with the inevitable "I'm sorry for your loss."

Zed laughed herself into the corner. They drove and Marlot smiled. After Friday's rain, the weather had been cooled in the city, but by the time they arrived, it seemed that July was readjusting its grip. They walked into the A.C. His mother's friends were waiting.

The agent had taken care of the day's proceedings and organized the funeral in accordance with his mother's wishes. She wanted to be buried because only the buried have headstones. "They're fun," she'd say, and Marlot had always wondered what she meant by that.

Her agent showed Marlot the headstone they had in mind. Handing Marlot her phone, he appraised the stone. A brown granite cylinder stuck deep into the earth. The stone was flecked with imperfections, natural to the rock type. They were made artificial by two gold bands that wrapped the base. The top of the stone was unpolished and Marlot laughed. He passed the phone to Zed.

Zed laughed as well, "Her grave's going to look like an ash tray." Mackenzie continued sheepishly. "It's not too late to get something different, but…"

Marlot shook his head, "But this is what she wanted."

*

Zed liked the funeral far more than the pre-funeral. While the pre-funeral had its accommodations, small sandwiches for example, she could only eat so many before it stopped being a good excuse to remove herself from conversation. Marlot, despite himself, spoke with the men and women who approached him regarding the passing of his "genius matriarch."

Zed stood by his side at first, but after the first couple of presuppositions regarding their relationship status, she found it easier to interact with the space on her own terms. Marlot did not mind. Apparently, as he mentioned to Zed, he needed to practice being nice even when he didn't necessarily want to be, "I should be more grateful."

She found his post-therapy self-righteousness almost more annoying than his grating personality. She grimaced when he said, "I'm happy to have had the time we were given," and excused herself after he used the word "blessed."

Pulling him aside after numerous fans passed by, she told him that therapy is not about change so much as it is growth.

Marlot shrugged and said, "Maybe I'm just growing so fast it seems like change."

Zed pursed her lips.

Marlot laughed.

At least he's not completely in the stratosphere, she thought. If anything, today functioned as a great opportunity to own himself, a process which he appeared to be enjoying. Zed considered networking.

Looking around the lobby, a varied collection of people moved with the gravity of mortality. How softly they sipped their teas and nibbled their sandwiches. How sternly they looked upon one another. Only Marlot appeared progressively more upbeat as the congregation competed to express their sorrow graciously. She watched them as a man approached from the side.

"Friend of the deceased?" he asked.

Zed turned and nodded, "Yes, I suppose I am."

"I'm sorry for your loss."

Zed bobbed her head, "Yeah." He continued to stand on ceremony.

"Can I help you?" she asked.

The man reached out a hand, "My name is Carlaw."

"Pleasure," Zed shifted in her platforms.

Carlaw's hair wisped about his head.

Zed looked over for Marlot, but the ladies he'd spoken to were now speaking to Mackenzie. Marlot was nowhere to be seen.

"I don't know about you, but I'm not so sure about the son," he chortled.

Zed affected an "hmm" sound.

"Personally, I can't stand him,"

Zed turned to see Marlot within a step of them. "Hi," he said loquaciously, "I'm the son, absolute pleasure."

Zed flushed, Marlot, it seemed, quite enjoyed being the centre of conversation. He reached an arm to Zed and bubbled, "Mind if I steal her away?" and Zed, despite herself, laughed and looped her arm in his. "To the casket!" Marlot exclaimed, as the greying Carlaw watched them run.

*

In the viewing room they separated.

"What is up with you?" She smiled. Her eyes shook around their sockets. They scanned his face, and he looked about the room with a grin.

"I don't know," he laughed, "Fuck, I shouldn't be laughing," he slapped his hand over his mouth, "or cursing, but… I feel so random," he said with an inflection.

Zed laughed, "No! No, you shouldn't, you'll have to do a better job of faking once the procession starts."

Marlot made a frown, "Like this?"

She studied him, "Yes, much better."

They had turned to face each other during the exchange. She smelled like vanilla and rose petals. Marlot blinked, "Maybe we should…?" He extended an open hand.

They both made note of how their fingers were not interlaced. Just two friends. Two people approaching a mother's casket. The casket was closed because Marlot said goodbye a week ago and saying goodbye twice was not going to help him. They stood before it and Marlot gripped one of the metal bars that wrapped the casket.

He let go of Zed's hand with his left and placed it next to his right. Zed gave him space. He appeared to whisper something, or perhaps change his breathing. Zed walked along the outside of the room and watched his face with a glance. His eyes were closed, and he took large intentional breaths that increased in pace over time. After several minutes his breathing slowed, and she approached him from the elbow.

He looked over at her quickly and then brought his head back to the casket. Then back at her.

They found a seat. Nodding to the manager of the Park Slope Hilton, Marlot took a chair beside Zed and waited for people to filter in. Soft, end-of-movie music played through the loudspeakers. Marlot's hand knuckled white in Zed's as they waited for the service to commence.

Mackenzie approached on the pulpit and its microphone. Marlot watched her. She gave several can-you-believe-it, looks, accompanied with a mouthed *thank you* to various people she recognized. Eventually she started talking. She offered her right hand to Marlot in reference and said a few words about love. Marlot nodded but mostly gazed at a position, just high and right of her left shoulder. Sometimes his butt squirmed in his seat.

"… if you'd like to say a few words." The room turned toward Marlot who continued to stare vacuously. Zed leaned into his ear, "Hey, you doing, okay?" Marlot nodded slowly, "Because I think it's your turn to speak." He looked around at the room. Zed yelped. In his anxiety Marlot over-squeezed her hand, and he let go apologizing.

An embarrassed Zed said, "No it's quite alright," and he let go of her hand. The room followed him as he walked. Where was his sparkle now? He coughed first and had a sip of Mackenzie's water. "I am so grateful…" he began. The room breathed around him.

"Thank you all for being here. I… It has been my pleasure meeting the many who have come to adore my mother." He paused.

Some people in the middle rows rustled pamphlets and squeaked in their seats.

"Excuse me," he had another sip. "Now that she is gone, I have had to figure out a lot of things for myself. It is not a secret that I have been disinherited by the late Marlot, but it is a secret that I have been made scared by my own fragility. She was more than my mother. She was a caretaker, my writing partner, my wall against the things that make life hard… I think I still found life hard, but more because of the things I did to make it that way. I wanted to feel sad for a time. I don't think she ever knew how to deal with that."

"When she got sick… The day before, she was healthy… I don't know how it happens. I mean, I know how it happens," he said with an awkward laugh, "you know, with the smoking and all…" Zed looked up encouragingly. He was rambling. He exhaled.

"Sorry." He recollected.

"It's weird when your mother becomes famous. Your whole life you feel like it's your turn to make something happen. When something happens for your parent, for your mom, when you're an adult… When her priorities shift to include a world outside being your mother… It's different. It's weird when she becomes famous for something that would kill her. She did, in fact, live large with her diagnosis. At times, I think I resented her for it. But she was a woman first. I think I still struggle to remember that. To me she was my mom."

Tears were streaming now. "I'm sorry." Zed had also begun to ache.

"I think many people look at my mom and see a refutation of death, but in the end…" A shadow crossed his brow. He wanted to say he hated her for quitting. But he didn't.

"Thank you." He returned to his seat.

*

At four, the office empties. Some come late and stay late, and some come early and leave early, but few came at four and stayed 'til midnight. Tonight, she'd sit alone, but it was quiet and her head, though tired, needed occupation. The coffee in her mug jiggled as she typed.

Calvin offered Zed a smile on his way out, but Zed was consumed by her screen. She switched between her browser and her calendar as she learned to write the code required for her master schedule. He left her to the space.

The hours passed quickly. She was almost fluid enough with the code for it to feel therapeutic. Her phone buzzed. Marlot texted her, "Thank you." She flipped it and placed it to the side.

By eleven Zed had finished. She'd make up the extra hour in the morning.

*

In the morning, she did not wish to make up that extra hour. Day screamed through her window, and she groaned. She pulled away from the sheets and she smelled the scent of her breath in the stagnant air. July… she thought. Her funeral wear fermented on the floor. She hung it up on a hanger and put it in front of the kitchen fan. She'd have to wear it again tomorrow.

Zed showered and dressed in her old dress pants and a crop top. She pulled her hair back and doused it with dry shampoo.

On the train, she could have slept an hour. Still, she relished her ten minutes before walking the rest of the way to the office. Calvin smoked outside and she waved, and he waved back. She was sure they'd talk at lunch.

As the hallway met the elevator, Mr. Mooney drifted into view. Then he walked directly to meet her feet. His slight, but imposing frame peered down on her from his vantage.

"Zed, I'd like to see you at lunch today." She gulped. "Please meet me at Conference Room B at 11:30. Do not bring food, you may eat at your desk afterwards."

Zed found her voice, "Okay."

He squinted at her.

"Yes, Sir." She coughed.

Appeased, he left her. Calvin made a whistling noise from behind. It sounded like a falling mortar. Zed turned to look at him.

He smiled, "Another meeting with bossman…"

"And a third this afternoon." She finished.

"What's it about?"

"I don't know." She thought of killing Mooney.

"Well, they can't fire you," he laughed. He seemed so confident. Her implicit "why" stared back through her eyebrows. "You just talked about the pay gap. They'd look terrible if they fired you the Tuesday after your confrontation.

Her heart slowed. "You're right, you're right," she paused to collect herself. "How goes the search?"

"The job search?" Calvin laughed sardonically. He proceeded to tell her about his weekend. In short, it was fine. Nothing yet.

They parted and Zed poured coffee before placing her butt in the seat she'd left only hours before. Still, she smiled. After three months, her calendar approached completion. Still, she missed her clothing.

By 11, Zed had finished what had become her beta version of the new calendar. This fortified her heart for the eventual meeting. Deliverable in hand, she met in Conference Room B at 11:25. A minute later, her notepads, pens, and an adapter buttressed her laptop. The next minutes ticked by slow. At 11:30 she thought maybe he wouldn't come. Her heart began to beat faster. Finally, a figure appeared in the doorway, and she turned, stern, before a laugh escaped her. It was only Matilda.

Matilda smiled and waved, but her brows antagonized her smile with some hidden discomfort.

"I thought you were Mr. Mooney," Zed admitted.

Matilda laughed as the gold-rimmed spectre appeared behind her.

*

Marlot woke late on Tuesday. Despite the mounting pressure to find a new place, he moved slow to do anything about it. It felt like eviction was unlikely, much less inevitable, and the prospect of storing or selling his mother's things seemed too cumbersome to manage.

He checked his phone, but Zed still hadn't messaged back. All he'd said was, "Thank you," but he felt she could react or something. He brought his laptop into the kitchen and considered writing cover letters. After a while he found himself rereading his subway scene.

"The train is quiet in the mornings..."

A little on the nose... He rubbed his temples. He turned toward poetry instead. "It's easier," he'd tell Zed on reflection. Easier to get back into.

*

The conference room was quiet. Not still, but almost immobile. Mr. Mooney removed his glasses and their soft clatter cut the air as much as anything. Matilda's hands interlocked her fingers. She squeezed at the knuckle. Zed felt she was hosting the meeting.

"So, how can I help?" Zed asked.

She looked into Mooney's eyes. They did not shiver in their sockets. Instead, they bore holes through their opponent. But he blinked and cleared his throat.

"As per our conversation last week, we've decided to increase your pay as to match the efforts you put into our company." Zed nodded. "In fact, despite our oversight, we're impressed with your work. To teach yourself any kind of code in response to a problem that you identified is impressive." He paused for effect.

Matilda frowned despite the news. Mooney maintained his quiet stare.

"We're given to understand that your calendar is almost complete?"

"Yes, I have the beta here."

"Wonderful, then you'll be able to start immediately."

"Start what?" Zed asked.

"Well, where…" Mooney paused. Matilda offered a half-hearted, you're-my-boss sort of laugh, then swallowed. Mooney cleared his throat, "California."

*

Zed resisted her initial inclination. "I'm not going to take it," she thought.

Still, she said nothing. Instead, he went on frowning. He exhaled and his lips flapped as he did so. An implicit "fuck" languished, but he looked upon her with a smile that felt, to him, courageous.

"When would you go?"

"Two weeks," she replied.

He rubbed his hand through his hair and his hair tumbled about his eyebrows.

"Have you decided if you'll take it?"

"It's what I've waited for."

"But California…"

"I know."

"West coasters," Marlot smirked sheepishly.

Zed laughed. Marlot frowned unconsciously.

"I am happy for you." He paused, "But I will miss you."

"Are you thinking of staying in the city?" Zed replied.

Marlot had not considered the alternative. "Yeah. Where else would I go?" He half-laughed, nervous, and Zed nodded. Marlot became stern in his study of their table. Maybe full-time employment could be pulled from the grain itself.

"I might not be able to stay."

"The city's not going anywhere," Zed offered, and he looked at her in the way she looked at Calvin earlier that evening.

"Is the city a place people come back to?"

They left the bar tipsier than anticipated. Marlot stopped asking questions. So, Zed asked if he was alright.

"Yeah," he said.

Zed groaned. "Come on! Get off it! We don't even know what's going to happen!"

Marlot laughed, "You're right. You're right." A big sigh followed. "But I cannot pretend to not be sad about it."

At least he was smiling. Zed smiled back and Marlot stopped walking and turned to look at the city. They had not watched where they were going. The city grew out of the river and Zed remembered her first day among the buildings. She remembered her Super and the bike ride over the bridge. She remembered stopping in the middle and remembered that this would be her first memory of the city. It was.

Marlot did not know what he was thinking. The water glimmered but he did not think of the city. He did not think of where he'd have to move or the job, he hoped awaited him. Instead, he thought of Zed's moving. Then he stopped thinking about Zed. His thoughts had gotten away from him. It was okay, she began walking.

The streets were quiet for a Tuesday, and they walked arm in arm toward somewhere in Bed-Stuy. Neither had a lot to say. They purchased wine from the corner and bagged it and sipped it as they smoothed an otherwise strenuous forty-eight hours.

Eventually, Zed stopped walking.

"What is it?" Marlot asked. His picture of her face kept swinging up and left. He corrected with his eyes, and yet upwards they dragged.

"We're here."

"Where else would we be?" Marlot bubbled and Zed looked at him sardonically. "We're here: at my house," Zed spelled for him.

The iron railings, and the green bicycle permanently locked to it drew Marlot's gaze up the stoop into her home.

"Oh…" Marlot felt Zed watching him. He busied himself making visual conversation in the action taken to perceive her residence. But it was just a building. And in short order, he'd seen it.

He looked back down at her. Did she always look so directly? Her eyes flicked about his corners, and then about his eyes. How quickly the lights were streaking. Too much time had passed in silence. Their evening was about to end. He could see her throat swallowing that very sentiment in preparation for departure, and yet Marlot could barely bear it. Her lips parted, on the cusp of something, but he struck first and faster:

"May I bum one of your cigarettes."

Her pulse began to die: seven minutes more. She passed him her package.

"Thank you." He looked awkwardly at the ground. Marlot didn't smoke. Zed knew that, but tonight they smoked together on the stoop outside her building.

*

Light filtered in through the window. Zed blinked and blinked again. A shiver shook her. She turned but he had gone.

*

He certainly found the morning. Checking his phone, the minutes ticked, and it became 6:30 on a Wednesday. The cars and trucks and bicycles made sounds, but it was the smell that consumed him: rose water.

*

The leather stretched in the dew and his feet dampened as he stood in the grass. It was good he left early. It was good that the cemetery was so close to home. A voice approached from behind, and Marlot turned to look back, but it was just the preacher. He spoke softly to the keeper.

Mackenzie pulled in on their heels and waved to Marlot from across the lawn. Overall, the mood was lighter today, and the proceedings directed more toward action than reflection.

This time last week, his mother had been dead two days. It had felt like a while. More than anything it felt like his mother's passing was no longer his priority. Instead, his life pushed on.

His phone buzzed: "Here."

Marlot deposited his phone back into his pocket and walked over to the parking lot. Zed was dressed as she had been the day before but wore boots instead of heels.

"The dew," she'd end up saying. "And the heat," he'd end up nodding, but first, he said hello. She, with her top half in the car said "Hey," casually and without circumstance. A quick, "One minute" re-cemented their friendship as he waited for her.

"For the headstone."

She retracted from the car with a bouquet of daffodils. "I was thinking Asphodel," she began, "but that seemed a little on the nose."

Marlot laughed.

"Hey, I'm sorry about last night, and slipping away in the morning, I didn't…"

"No, no, you're all good." Zed interrupted. She continued, "It was fine, we are fine."

The sun began to fry the lot.

"Maybe we can talk in the shade." Zed suggested. Marlot nodded but didn't know what he was to say. Fortunately, the preacher had begun calling them over. Marlot thanked God for the dead.

*

The service began and the preacher said things and Marlot enjoyed the delivery. Like a priest at a wedding, the man struck Marlot as cute, if anything, and sweet for speaking over the dead.

Marlot waved away the chance to speak again when asked by the preacher. He instead motioned for motion in the proceedings which proceeded as expected.

The grave digger or grounds keeper or whomever it is that lowers coffins into the earth, lowered the coffin into the earth. Thirty people watched her disappear into the dirt.

Her coffin hit the dirt floor. Zed threw her flowers on top of the coffin. Other people brought flowers which they, then, too, threw onto the casket. It was pretty but the sun burned. Mackenzie cried uncontrollably. Perhaps the death of Ms. Marlot's profitability caught up with her. Difficult to say. Especially at the rate with which it ended.

Burial goers evaporated and her death was sealed on a line that agreed to fulfill the credit paid in the burying of his mother. Dead, but now dead and gone. What's more, it was sunny.

Zed squinted from the far end of the park and Marlot joined her.

*

Zed dropped him off at the office. She squinted through the driver's side window at the building and made a neutral addition to the silence that pervaded the scene.

"Hmm" she hmmed with an upward inflection.

"What? I thought you'd be excited."

"It's therapy, not an award ceremony. I'm proud of you but what do you want from me?"

"Damn, okay," Marlot laughed. He felt uncertain, so he tried a joke, "Then you don't have to come in."

Zed missed it entirely. "I have to get to work anyway," she said. She whipped out of the bus lane and Marlot came through the doors of the office. He walked in with a buried mother and his first funeral speech. And Zed, he thought, as she sped to work down Broad.

Therapy is easier the second time. This time he nodded at the lady behind the desk and the man who let people into the offices behind the side door. This time there were fewer children and more adults and Marlot felt significantly less old for being there.

Once more his name was called. Clawson greeted him as before.

"I promise not to yell," Marlot said to lighten the mood.

Clawson did not respond, so he apologized more specifically. Clawson said, you do not have to apologize, and their session began. He sat in the chair across from Clawson.

Clawson asked Marlot how his week was going. By the time he finished recounting all of his experiences, the time he had in the office had all but evaporated.

"How do you feel like you're doing?"

"Good, good," Marlot said. "I guess I haven't thought about it. A lot of the things I stressed over have ended."

"Have their departures left room for newer stresses?"

Marlot's smile retracted into a flatter face. "Yeah, I guess they have."

He paused to think about it. He thought of Zed, but didn't want to talk about her, yet.

"I might have to leave the city," he stated after some amount of time. Clawson leaned closer.

"I…" he sighed. "I…" another pause. "Fuck," he laughed at himself. "I may have to leave the city because I do not have enough money to stay here. I need a job. I'm not good at anything in particular. I have a job but the pay…" his fingers knotted and unknotted and knotted again. "Despite everything I think of, I need a job like yesterday if I hope to find a place to swing rent in the next two weeks."

He laid the topics out with his hands in front of the doctor. Dr Clawson replied, "Why do you want to stay?"

Nobody had asked him that.

Dr. Clawson continued. "It's expensive, small, poorly made, and dirty. The job opportunities, at the jobs you're looking at, come to people who already know people, and, while people already know you, few will take your reputation as a gold star, so," she paused for effect, "Why do you want to stay in the city?"

This singularly directed tirade came almost without emotion. It did not feel like she didn't believe in him: belief seemed irrelevant to the statement. Instead, she simply mentioned truths. Marlot leaned back in his chair. He could see his reason for staying very easily if he thought about it. He continued to look up and around the ceiling as he searched for some better sounding answer.

Without one, he looked back at Dr. Clawson. Her eyes threaded through the space between his seams. He pushed back into her eyes, but this had the opposite effect of what he wanted. Feeling vulnerable, he picked a reason. "Writing, I suppose." Clawson made a hmm sound. She sat up in her chair and took off her glasses.

She looked at Marlot in the eyes and his pulse quickened. "There are writing jobs all over the country Marlot, so why this city?"

Marlot felt giddy and terrified, but Clawson offered space for him to think about it. "Let's meet again next week. Maybe you can tell me what's on your mind then." She replaced her glasses on her nose and smiled. Marlot nodded and said that sounded fine.

*

He bought cookies on his way home. He wanted to offset his desire to smoke, but he passed a deli that sold flower before he made it back to Grove Street.

"Is this by the eighth?"

The lady said it was. "This is what we've got, and this is what it costs."

He smoked a block down from his corner. In sitting, he watched his city dim. Parents and neighbors began playing dominoes and cards while children danced in the water from the hydrant.

He could almost count his steps, now: leaving. Really, am I leaving? A hopelessness gripped his heart. A solitude in his life's design became apparent. If not my home, then where? If not the city, then where? If not writing, then what? If not Zed... he stopped. If not Zed, then why?

The screaming screamed around him. There was so much joy. He smoked on the corner and waited for the street to darken.

*

Once more it was morning. "Again..." he thought, agitated. The Facebook forums that called for roommates responded on occasion, but they required funding, money, he did not have following the rent hikes in the city.

45% of apartments are rent controlled, he read, and yet... perhaps... But, if not here, then where? He called Zed and asked about her place, but she had not determined whether she was going.

*

Zed started her morning in a similar strain of stress. Where Marlot had the day sorted in a couple hours for the magazine, her moderately inflexible nine-hour shifts gave her little time for reflection. Twelve days until California. Her calendar bulged in the interim: demonstration, demonstration, submission, and supervised execution.

What she spoke about hypothetically came across now as a $175,000 job offer. She could even hear her insolence. "What about my art?" The words sounded hollow. Calvin sighed and gave a sad if not envious smile.

"You will go because you have to."

She frowned nervously.

"Zed," he asked, "what about this actually scares you?"

"Am I not giving up?" she replied.

Calvin straw sucked air, dramatically underscoring his, "On what?" follow up.

"On my life? Is this not failure?"

"Failure does not come with a $130,000 raise."

"I just want to stay here."

Calvin sighed, "Zed, I want to say what people say: that whatever you choose will be the right call and that life is long and you can make it no matter what, but..." He paused on himself. "But it is not like that. It is not easy, these opportunities do not come, I am not going to be offered this position, and you know what, I think you're being stupid by thinking that going corporate in this country, given your salary, given our salary, and given the price of our living... You could buy a fucking house. Don't stay because it's easy."

Zed teared up. She nodded and shook her head. Calvin frowned. He shook his head and place an arm around her.

"No, you're right, it's fine, I am fine. I should get back to the office."

Her text from Marlot waited. How slow the last week had been. In days, too much had happened. Marlot called. She sent it straight to voicemail.

*

He felt still. An email blipped on his screen: The Wright Fit at 101 Warren Street, request for an interview.

Marlot emailed back, softening the tone he thought with.

"Hello Mike," they did not know his name preference, "thank you for your prompt response, are you available for an interview this afternoon at 2:00? Best, Will"

Marlot fired back immediately. Yes, of course, and offered along his number.

He spent the next hours transcribing an interview for the magazine. The mind-numbing nature of the work gave him peace and pause. The phone rang accordingly. Will did not know his mother.

They talked for half an hour. Marlot leaned into his time with climbing as experience for this Luxury Fitness Attendant position. "Lots of training experience," he lied. Will appeared most interested in his capacity for lifting seventy-five pounds.

"Something that interested me about your company was the room for vertical movement."

Will appeared to nod through the phone. Marlot could come by in the morning.

*

It seemed, to Zed, that the opportunity came as a result of his anxiety about retaining her in his office. She held firm her reflection. They mirrored each other's sternness, passing in by the office printer.

*

Zed would not answer his calls. What had been such a good burial was quickly turning into a disparate reality. Marlot did not have friends to lose, a thought he thought in the time between 2:30 and bed. He played chess on the computer. A friend texted him to say she was in town. He texted Zed and asked if she was free tonight. By 4:00 she texted:

"Can't" or won't. She could only handle her emotions. How much did he really need from her anyway. Where was her support? Where was his offer to help her about the move? No. Better to plan. Better to look at places in California. Better to leave work early. No time for boys.

She snapped her laptop shut. Matilda looked over and Zed said, "I'll be working from home."

"Is everything alright, Zed?" despite her control, she had come out of herself a bit. Her voice cracked, and she replied that all was well, that she just had to figure out this California thing. Matilda's mouth creased. "It doesn't need to be alright," she said, and Zed replied, "I'm fine, Matilda!" and left the office.

Her walk home was peppered with frustrations. The train had closed again, and Zed shrieked coming out of the platform, "Fuck this train and fuck this city." Being angry helped.

Sweat poured from her brow by the time she made it back to her apartment. Her roommates talked loudly at one another about whether or not they had in fact made plans to see one of their families for dinner.

"I'm busy, Grace!"

"With what? What could you possibly have going on?"

Post-retrograde was hitting, Zed thought. Marlot had joked about it a month ago.

Zed looked remiss on where she was a month ago. It had been a nightmare punctuated by brief reprieves described primarily through surprising acts of sweetness. She thought about Marlot. But then she sighed and went into her room.

*

They met at the Peculiar Pub in the Village because that's where Marlot took people who were visiting the city.

She was already high. Marlot felt destructive.

"How are things?" and she told him.

"Good and bad," and she winked at him as she said it.

"How about you? Are you as sardonic as I remember?"

Marlot scoffed, "No, I have someone for that." and Lydia leaned in ever closer.

"Oh really? Then where are they?" she replied.

Marlot wished he hadn't said anything, and she laughed, "It's fine, you're not the love of my life either. We're just having a chat."

Their chat lasted longer than he had anticipated. What started as offloading culminated in drinks Marlot could not afford. She smiled and he purchased them anyway.

"Sounds to me you're in love with her," and Marlot laughed and said that was ridiculous in the way that people do when a stranger undresses them. Lydia continued, "It's only ridiculous because you'd rather things happen without your asking but guess what..." She leaned in very closely, "If you don't tell her, no one will."

"She's moving to California, Lydia."

"She *might* be moving to California."

"Even if I did love her,"

Lydia grinned.

"Which I don't."

Lydia nodded sarcastically.

"Then what? Is it fair of me to tell her?"

Lydia sipped and shrugged, "Depends how badly you need her to know."

They smoked on the train. 1:30 am came on quick and some interim period between stations covered conversation in ranges. "Where are we going?" Lydia laughed, and Marlot said, "I don't know, wherever you want to go."

They had agreed on sex when he'd called her. It was not like how it was with Zed, "I mean we didn't even do anything," he'd said at the bar, and Lydia said they had slept together. He supposed that was true, "but we just slept," and she nodded, voguing sympathy, with a tempered expression.

But that felt like eons ago and now they were off the platform. "Where do you want to go?"

"Well," Marlot said uncomfortably, "we could play pool,"

"Let's walk and see how we're feeling,"

Inevitably, they walked past Marlot's. Inevitably they walked inside, and she asked for water.

He brought it along and she pulled a pre-roll from her pocket, "Bought it in Nolita," she offered anecdotally. They smoked quietly in the yard.

Eventually they did go inside. Marlot giggled and then apologized as he remembered the state of his room.

"Sorry about the mess." She nodded and looked at his walls.

"Why are they so empty?"

"It helps me write. I don't have to… it doesn't matter, I should get paintings or something."

She said she liked his curtains. They sat on his mattress. He gulped at his water as she took off her shoes.

"I'm gonna go fill these up." His head ballooned under the pressure of his high. He sucked down another cup, refilled hers and his and walked back to the bedroom. She lay back and stared at her phone as he handed her the water.

"Did you see the new *Spiderman?*" What the fuck was he talking about? Did she really want to touch him?

Her boots and socks sat in the corner. She sipped at her water and pulled Trident from her pocket. She offered him the gum and he took it, and they chewed it, and she sat up so that their faces were closer to one another. He looked at their knees. They were already touching. She could have moved away if she had wanted to. But she didn't.

"Are you in love with someone?" he wanted to ask, but he had already lent in. She smelled of incense and weed and perfume. She smelled like high school. She smelled of those aspirations he held before he knew Zed and before his mom wrote commentary or was famous. Her lips tasted like strawberries.

*

Zed's anguish reached resolution. Despite her intense frustration she calmed and found solace in her painting. She layered and chipped away at an older canvas. She found she painted Marlot. It did not look like Marlot, at least Marlot's skin wasn't made of blues or reds or greens, but his expression: those critical eyes, that insipid dissatisfaction, they were his. She tired of this. It was quickly becoming morning. 2:15 becomes 4:00, and she thought about going to bed. Instead, she called back Marlot.

*

His phone rang. He offered Lydia a rag to which she said, "Wow, what a gentleman," and he picked up his cellphone. His heart froze and she looked at him.

"Is it…?"

He nodded.

She laughed,

Marlot fumbled and he replaced the phone on the nightstand.

Lydia cackled in his sheets. He smiled, sheepish. The phone buzzed on the table.

"Well, aren't you going to answer it?"

"No, of course not, I want you to stay the night."

Her golden eyes shimmered. "I'm on my way out anyway. You do whatever you have to."

*

She accepted his Face Time. A very messy looking Marlot stared back at her as she finished brushing her teeth.

"Hey, is everything alright?" he asked.

She spat into the sink. "Yeah,"

"Why did you call?"

Zed didn't really know why she called. I guess to talk, "Do you want to come over?" Marlot nodded. "Okay, I'll see you then." She hung up the phone.

*

Marlot showered as fast as he could. His room was in greater disorder than before, but he had enough clean clothes to make it over to hers. He pocketed his weed. Best to not do anything too outrageous. He biked quickly in the evening.

She buzzed him in. "Bring your bike inside if you want." He elected to leave it out. His steps kept pace with her heart's beating, and soon he'd entered through the door.

"Fire escape?" she offered, and he joined her on the landing. She pulled a cigarette from her package and while Marlot didn't smoke, that was increasingly untrue.

"Drunk?" she asked, "and high," he replied, why was it so hard to talk to her sometimes.

His implicit, "How's work?" followed and her lips thinned. A taut line of smoke pulled from them.

She told him about her conversation with Calvin and Marlot kept refocusing on her nose until he could see her clearly. He came in as she finished. Then he sat silently for a while.

She looked over at him. He seemed to be thinking of something.

"What is it?"

He apologized; I'm just trying to think of how I'd like to phrase it. He thought of therapy.

Zed nodded.

Marlot sighed and looked up at the moon. It was full. On a Thursday no less. It would soon disappear.

"I think Calvin is right."

Zed blinked.

Marlot continued, "I don't know if I necessarily agree with all he had to say, but you can't," he stammered, "you can't not get paid this money. Obviously, you can, and you can push fashion, but you make street wear, Zed. What are you doing on the east coast? Your clothes, they belong on artists, musical artists, in videos and in photos and I don't know how this is a toss-up for you."

Zed nodded; she had reached the same conclusion herself in her apartment on her newspapers on her floor pouring paint into her paintings.

"You are a talented designer," and I do believe in your ability to make artwork for you, but you will still be in fashion out there and you'll have money. You'll have so much fucking money. You will be able to produce yourself if you so choose." She nodded but looked down at her feet.

Marlot thought about what to say. "I... I love you so much Zed. You know I will miss you and you know," he added with a laugh, "but to not go because you're scared... I don't know."

The question struck her. There was no real answer. He smiled. She sighed. He replied, "Sometimes, we just have to do stuff that makes us uncomfortable."

She moved to sit next to Marlot. "Thanks."

She leaned her cheek against his shoulder, and he reciprocated by leaning his head against her scalp. They watched the sky turn into light.

*

Marlot fidgeted in the lobby.

"Are you comfortable?" The woman in the coat called from the desk.

"Yes, thank you." Marlot had not slept. He only left Zed's three hours ago. Between that walk, his coffee, shave, shower, dress clothes, and train, he had little time for anything other than the most basic interview preparations. His phone buzzed.

"Good luck!"

Marlot laugh-reacted. A man joined him in the lobby. His hair was shorn within a half inch of his scalp. He sweat faintly in the lobby.

"Michael?" he offered.

Marlot stood and greeted him. He was a tall man made short by his appearance: underwhelming, courteous, directed, dutiful, placid. Marlot shook his head and smiled.

"Hi, Will." Marlot put on his best face.

Will talked about The Wright Fit in the elevator.

"It started back in 2007," he began, and Marot became a reflection of Will's emotions. In a sense, they connected. "Don't forget to smile…"

The Wright Fit, as Will explained, was a company built for luxury residences. A celebrity, Jay Wright, "thus the name," Will explained, began the company to solve a problem: luxury amenities spaces not having luxury staff to work them. Marlot scratched an itch under his collar.

Will led him to a conference room. They sat down and Will began his cold open. "Look, it's an easy job, but you will need to do it perfectly." Marlot wrote down Will's words. His notebook took on information regretfully. His old notes flipped to the front, ideas for books and shows and movies and poems… and now: Jay Wright is the founder of The Wright Fit; there is a proper way to roll towels.

Will asked numerous questions that culminated in what he believed to be insightful. If you could meet three people, he asked, and Marlot answered. Will asked whether he thought Shakespeare was real or not, to which Marlot answered at length. Will nodded in the way someone does when they ask a question for the sake of asking it.

He smiled and said, "Good answer, I always ask this question because people who choose only living people lack imagination." Marlot considered this thought and disagreed but smiled and the man before him.

*

Marlot woke ten days before moving. An email blinked into his inbox, another from the magazine… He emailed back and pulled around his laptop. Today he was to write a climbing shoe review…

In his interviews for jobs, Marlot found his occupational output impressive. Many thought Marlot worked full-time because he told them that he did. When he told them about his output per week, they were impressed despite the fact that they thought he worked 40 hours a week.

Public speaking is easiest when you already know what you're talking about, he would think, a thought that came readily as his work was always off the top of his head. Sometimes they would do an interview or a longer form investigative piece and, in all cases, Marlot published nearly daily.

You're not a writer unless you publish...

He shut his laptop. At his best Marlot was a climbing writer, a title whose descriptor detracted from the subsequently described position. Even his title, editor, was made lesser by its qualifier.... Perhaps it's best not to say what you do for a living, he thought. Still, Marlot found himself explaining his existence.

*

"Are you sure you want to be a writer?" Zed leaned across the table. She asked this question periodically and Marlot could never tell if she remembered the last time, she'd mentioned it. She proposed it as a challenge, or that was how he interpreted it. When things were going well, he'd say yes and when things went poorly, he'd still say, yes, but he'd spent a lot more time thinking about it.

These days, Marlot did not feel like much of a writer. The email he received earlier described an error he made on an article about chalk absorptivity. Good Lord, he'd thought.

"I'm looking for work," he said to Zed. His eyes picked through the weeds growing through the sidewalk. He wondered how they stayed green in the sun.

"Why do you ask me that?"

"Is it an odd question to ask?"

"No. I guess it's not."

Zed sipped from her soda.

"But you ask it a lot."

"When was the last time I asked it?"

"I don't know. Is twice not strange?"

"I must have forgotten," Zed replied.

"Yeah."

A car crawled by. Marlot smelled the exhaust. He guessed her response was fair. What else was she to say?

Zed watched him recede. She sighed a great huffaw of a sigh and his knee bounced on the patio. He twitched his head toward her.

"It makes me think that you think that I don't want to be a writer."

"Do you?"

"Why? Why again?"

"Because we're talking about it, Marlot!"

The train thundered overhead. Marlot watched her return to her seat.

He wavered. "I want to be a writer."

"Then explain these last months to me. You stopped. You started smoking…"

"It's just weed…"

"Is it?" Her pitch increased.

"I had an interview yesterday."

"You already have a job!"

"It pays shit, Elizabeth!" He strung out every syllable.

"It pays shit… Have you tried being worth more than what they're paying you? You are 23 years old! What do you know? For the love of Christ, Marlot, you already have the job of your dreams and yet you languish in suffering for no one has noted your competition analytics as worthy of a Pulitzer. You can't even say that you want to be a writer. What is it that you want to do? Do you know? Or will you work some shit job and call that good?"

Her hands unclenched after the question.

Marlot stood and the chair tipped over onto to patio. It clattered.

"What the fuck is wrong with you? I just lost my mother. I'm doing just fine."

"That's shit and you know it. This isn't about her, Marlot."

Marlot ingested. Zed watched his eyes shift before she sighed herself.

*

Meredith's publisher emailed in the morning. Deborah Laurence Miller had read the article in the *Post*. She was interested in the second novel.

To Michael Marlot,

I saw your article in the Post: bastards. Still, I wondered about the second novel. Where did she end her composition? Jim didn't make it clear. I guess that was the point. Anyway, sorry for your loss.

Best,

Deborah Laurence Miller

He frowned at the text and looked up from his kitchen table. His mother's door stood in its sill, latched, and shadowed by the light coming from the hallway. He consciously moved his eyes away from the door and returned them to the laptop screen.

Where did she end her composition? Marlot had not checked. Her laptop was probably still charging in on the desk in front of the chair she'd pulled out or pushed in however much she had done so. He clicked open a new email. He wanted to say that there was nothing to be done, sorry, thank you and goodbye.

He wondered if that was fair. He would have to unpack his mother's room eventually. He would have to move shortly. It could not be helped. Between the funeral and burial, Zed, and Clawson, he had not moved from his original predicament. Even if this job shook out with The Wright Fit, his income would barely cover rent and food. It would not guarantee an apartment.

It dawned on Marlot he'd have to move or find twelve months' rent for a studio and pay it all up front. A studio cost quite a bit more than a room in an apartment. He closed the email and researched apartments nearby and not-so-nearby. $1600 was less than he'd expected. Almost twenty-grand… he frowned.

Hi Deborah,

Thank you for your condolences. I have not been able to bring myself to look through her files.

Regards,

Michael

An anxiety passed over him. It felt like expectation or opportunity evaporated in an instant, but there was no opportunity in another's work. How could he publish under his mother's name? What cause did he have to share his mother's cannon? Could they know? Would they care? Does it matter?

He felt silly for asking questions, and so he exited onto the patio behind his mother's bedroom. The shadowy door of her dormitory remained still. It remained untouched and yet he watched it. As though she might stumble out in a morning's disarray, squinting "Coffee," to which he'd laugh and say it's on the counter.

But it was not on the counter. He'd stopped buying coffee. Everything felt expensive. He jiggled the door into the back yard. His mother's ashtray was as she left it, if not damper, greener, for the days between her last cigarette and her publisher's email. He eased himself into the corroding iron and let his spine relax in the sun.

Still morning but still hot as well. He watched a plant grow from the planter in which she'd placed her butts. He wondered if it came from the tree overhead. Its leaves had begun changing into that almost-yellow summer color.

Zed called on the phone. He let it ring. He had forgotten about the night before. So much anger. She was right of course, but it hurt him to be seen as such a spectator. He felt he watched others' lives unfold while he waited for something, anything. The curtains moved in his mother's window.

He snapped his head to attention and for a moment caught a spectre, but it was only a shadow. Her AC unit hummed. How much they'd spent on refrigerating her empty room. Marlot sighed and stood and went back inside. The patio door squelched open on its weather stripping and Marlot took in his mother's door: heavy, white, wooden, with a brass knob that appeared only partially oxidized.

How we conjure spirits, he thought, but he placed his hand on the knob. His heart had begun beating louder now; like it does on the edge of a cliff where you could jump or not jump, but all your friends have jumped before. You want to jump. It seems right, but at the same time… what if you do it wrong? What if the dust can never settle in the same way? What if a rock has moved in the time between you and the person before you? What if something happens that you can't take back?

The latch split open. The knob felt cool in his hand. It pulled from the temperature of his mother's room... He pushed the door open.

In a moment, a rush of air and cool and wind shifted his hair, and he breathed what he thought could only be death, but again it was only air conditioning. And he stood on her carpet. And all of the things he remembered about her room were as she'd left them. The bureau was still wedged between the closet and the wall, while the AC unit burred happily, filtering what could have become musty air.

She had made her bed the day she died, and that made Marlot smile. Her laptop and her desk, a large, almost table like structure, took up most of the available space, while her bookshelves filled the inset brick that appeared intended for wall-mounted televisions.

He walked along the carpet and lifted her laptop from the table. He looked at where he'd sat only moments before, on the patio in the yard. Then he left her room altogether and returned to the kitchen table.

A deep sense of loneliness pervaded. How he had wanted there to be a spectre: a ghost, or memory, drifting through the halls. But there wasn't. He was alone. And all he could think was how right that seemed to him. He sat at the table and cried.

*

Zed woke up soaking wet. The sun from window has fallen on her comforter making for a net of shadows, under which, she slept. Of course, July in the mid-Atlantic is hardly crisp and so Zed peeled her sheets from her body with a groan. She regretted the way she'd spoken to Marlot, but only because she did not like seeing him upset. His character, she thought... to her he seemed a child.

Although she loved Marlot, she struggled with what that meant. To be all things to another person is heavy and not the task taken by best friends. At best it's taken by siblings, but to call their, whatever they were, a familial relation seemed insidious and perverse. Still, she could have controlled her tone. Then again, he could show some self-awareness. Why was it on her to moderate her feelings when he was being ridiculous? I am not your mother, she thought, and then some realization dawned. She shivered with ick.

Scrubbing in the shower helped, but not thinking about him helped more. She painted in her living room when Mooney called, and her heart did not jump. Instead, she answered,

"Hi, Zed speaking."

"Hello Ms. Carter."

Zed gave a start, "Calvin?"

"Yes," he laughed, "I'm afraid, today, I have been reduced to the role of executive assistant."

"Where are you?"

"At the office."

"It's Sunday."

"I know, but when he calls, I answer."

"Mooney?"

"Yes."

"Oh…" There was a pause

"Yeah, so anyway," he said leaning on the -*way*, "I am calling about California. You're booked for Monday, is that alright?"

"Yes, that's alright."

"Good, there are no other options, but I thought I'd frame it as a question."

Zed laughed, "Well, thank you Calvin."

"Don't thank me, I am merely an assistant working on a Sunday."

She could hear his grin through the phone. "Hardly *mere*, I'd say."

"And yet mere all the same. Anyway, this merely gorgeous, funny, and talented assistant must go before Mooney questions his ability to make phone calls, but I love you and wish you luck."

"Did he tell you where I am going?"

"Los Angeles?"

"No, yes, obviously, but am I to go straight to the office?"

He appeared to shrug, "I'll ask." The phone sat static a moment. Zed looked around her apartment. Grace started moving in the kitchen. The hair on her neck bristled... Perhaps it is time to go, she thought. Calvin returned to the line.

"Mr. Mooney says," Calvin cleared his throats, *"Naturally."*

Zed barked a laugh. "Thank you, Calvin."

"Of course, my dear. When you make it to the top, don't forget about me. Alright, I must run." Calvin hung up the phone.

Zed made happy movements in her room. Her fan cooled her from the shower. If she stood outside its range, the apartment felt insufferable. She would have to shower again. But for now, she had a day to pack and a place to go. How she'd dreamt of California.

*

"Sometimes I think about dying. It is not a new thought nor is it particularly pervasive. Things distract me and I will think of living, but only by its actions. I must submit my edits, or I must make my appointment, or my assignment is due tomorrow. Sometimes these thoughts were related and other times they weren't. It never seemed convenient.

As a child, I told my father, and my father told my mother and they both seemed upset. They said it is not your place to die, and I wondered what they meant. My dad said it meant I was too young to feel that way.

When you are young, that's all it takes. A quick concern, a direction that says, "This future is not for you." There is too little to compare. Alright, you say, or I said, and then you are older and in school.

In school these thoughts become aesthetic. The books and the movies and the people who die by suicide or otherwise, who pass long before their time and are simultaneously described by that passing, pervade the conscience. How sexy to be misunderstood. But aren't we all, I thought, and in high school, so it seemed. Maybe I'm not lonely.

When my parents died, I was an adult. A young adult with a lover who held my hand at their funerals. They almost passed together and the boy I knew for a year or less replaced them: a reason. Why not keep on living, I thought, and yet it seemed my father must have thought about dying. He passed second. His brother thought he'd died of heartbreak. I wondered if I could love someone like that.

In the autumn after school, he proposed. He said he didn't mean to, and I wondered what he meant by that. He said, I thought it would make you happy.

For a time, it made me happy. We were qualified and young and had a wedding to plan. We had jobs and we had a house and I wondered if this was what I'd waited for. He told me about his plans.

"For now, I am just me, but together we might be something."

"What if we don't become anything?" I'd asked.

He smiled, "We already have."

It turns out he was right. By that time, I was pregnant. We moved our dates up so I could keep the wedding dress. You can see the bump in the video if you watch it. When he laughs, he looks like Michael. We did not know that would be the case. I don't know how to write about pregnancy, but it was more than depression. It was... dramatic. So rarely does a person feel so desperately alive.

I liked being alive when I was pregnant. He answered my quest for persistence. A distraction I could not shake. A distraction that risked my life. A conscious, consequential reason to keep breathing. I read a lot over that time.

After consummation I earned a job at Harper-Collins. Women in the workforce, they implied. It frustrated them when I took maternal leave so soon. Such is life, I thought. They would not fire the pregnant lady.

I read and released several works I had not anticipated becoming best sellers. It seemed that the best-selling books were just well produced. The rest, well, there were some that read well too. For a while I thought this was what I wanted. After I had Michael, I realized I had done most of the things I had set out for. I had a child and a husband and a job and a home. I lived precisely where I meant to and yet... pervasive, this feeling of entrapment.

Robert stayed at home, at first, and I spent my time in the office. Michael didn't mind, or if he did, there was nothing we could do about it. My job was consistent, Robert's would not suffer from his absence. We woke up in the mornings and Michael slept between us.

By the time he'd finished reading, the light had faded. His unintentionally emotional afternoon became brighter, lighter than what he'd remembered. The words she'd never shared, he thought, and he wondered about his own emotions.

It seemed to go on endlessly. She had never spoken about her parents, but Marlot had never asked. He had wondered about his grandparents but only learned they'd died long ago. As a grandchild to the deceased, he did not think about them deeply. Only in photos would he try to find himself in their faces, and it was always unclear whether he could. Of course, other things would happen.

He called Zed in the midst of his reading, but only got her voicemail. He wanted to talk about himself, about his book, his mother's book: or diary, or whatever 50,000 words can be. But he called and said that he was wrong, that he was insecure, that he was sorry. How often must he be sorry, he wondered? At least as often as his mistakes, he thought. He considered Carlaw's quotes.

"What exactly are your values?"

His phone buzzed on the table. A rush of dopamine joined a feeling of pain. She wrote back his call-in lower case: hey.

He replied the same. How tactical texting had become.

She called him and he began apologizing, but he could tell her mind was elsewhere because she told him that she had not even thought about it.

"Well," he said sheepish, "I'm sorry anyway. What are you up to tonight?"

"Packing mostly. Calvin called this morning; I'm going to California."

Marlot's throat squeezed down some words he would regret and, instead, he said, "Oh!" in a disappointed sort of way. Zed was silent on the other end. Marlot gulped down his squeezing throat, "Oh, that sounds lovely, Los Angeles?"

Zed rolled a pencil between her thumb and forefinger. They'd been over this. "Yeah, should be good."

Marlot tried to think of something to say but could not and resolved to say goodbye. As he meant to, Zed interrupted and asked him what he was up to.

"I found some of my mother's writing. It's weird."

"What is it about?"

"I don't know. It's about her, I guess. I don't think it's about anything else."

"Is it good?"

"It is interesting."

"Doesn't that mean bad?"

He laughed, "I guess, but not this time. It's just weird. I don't know. I can send it to you if you'd like: for the ride. Or you could come over." His heart wrenched as he said it. Such a dispossession of power, prostrating himself for this girl he needed to not hate him.

"Yeah, alright, I'll be over."

"Cool."

"See you."

Zed hung up the phone. Why had things become so awkward so forced. Not days ago, it was effortless and now she says a few strict words and that's that. Maybe it was just a moment. But Zed suspected it was more than that. A thought entered and her heart quelled, but when she squinted, she could look past it.

*

The oven roasted. She could hear the snapping of oil as its splashed amongst his potatoes. Its heat battled with the air conditioning giving every ten feet a different climate.

"What about Rosé?" he asked.

"God yes," and he brought it into the den.

The den and the kitchen were, in many ways, a single room, but the space had been styled in such a way that it appeared separate, almost detached. His mother had installed doors to close it out if the occupants desired.

Zed turned from the window, from the street, and accepted the glass he poured in the air, and she looked up at him and he looked back at her, and they said nothing. Marlot drank his glass and poured another. The wine imbibed him with a fleeting self-consciousness that he referenced as he sat in the chair across from her.

"I am sorry," he said again.

"For the love of God, Marlot, I'm over it. You don't have to keep apologizing."

"I just feel it might be best to talk about it."

"I don't know what I'd want to say."

Marlot sighed, exasperated. He rarely found himself on this side of improper communication. "I am sorry things are weird. I took it personally. I am afraid of the way you see me."

Zed softened in his confession.

"I am afraid you'll leave, and now you're actually leaving."

"Well, just for a couple of days."

"Until"

"I possibly move there for good..." she finished. It was not hard to see his point.

"I just don't want you to cut me out." He paused. Then, "Fuck, I feel fucking neurotic."

Zed smiled into her glass, tipping it back and raising an eyebrow. Marlot looked deadpan at her. She laughed into her glass and wine sprayed into and then out of her glass onto her face and the floor.

Marlot laughed as well.

"Stahp," she said nasally, smiling. "Ugh, it burns." Marlot watched some wine trickle out of her nostril and doubled over all over again. The tension relaxed and he grabbed her a napkin.

She held the napkin to her nose.

"I'm not going to cut you out, you know…" Her nose inhibited her articulation. She wiped and sniffed and made a *MWUAH* sound and motion with her mouth. She inhaled again and looked at him.

"I'm just worried about you."

Marlot lifted and sank. He thought of all the things he could say. Then he thought some more, until finally, "Thank you."

She breathed. He breathed. She breathed. He said, "I'm worried too."

His hands strained against the strength of the chair. "I…" he faltered. "I think I'm going to have to move."

"Well, you're definitely going to have to move," she replied, and they looked around the apartment. It felt almost like they'd grown up together. But in a sense, they had. They were, he thought, and she might have thought it too as they stood and grabbed plates and napkins for dinner.

The potatoes and the roast they surrounded sizzled. Zed complimented Marlot and he laughed and said, "Try it first," in the self-consciously abashed way that people communicate with one another after an interlude of soul baring.

Eventually the food cleared away and they were drinking and then they were smoking.

"I normally wouldn't, but then again…."

"It won't be yours for much longer now," she laughed. And he joined her in laughing. Before dinner finished, they transitioned from the Rosé to a Moscato to realizing they had empty glasses. They grabbed a third bottle and Marlot mentioned the roof. It was a perfect night for roofing.

The stars were invisible behind a thick layer of clouds, but the city's light would have been more than enough to block it anyway. A smoky haze seemed to settle at the highest points of the city's skyscrapers and Marlot's heart beat as Zed approached him and then the edge.

The sloping roof was designed to carry water efficiently into one of the building's many gutters, but from the roof it made a ramp that a person could walk up if they chose. Zed stood upon the precipice.

Do you ever think about jumping? She asked.

Marlot looked up from his laptop, I think everybody does.

Zed noted the attractive way his eyes sunk into the bones of his skull. The computer cast light from below. It reminded her of flashlights held under chins by camp counselors who told stories.

Marlot cleared his throat.

It was our second Fall. The birth and the bed clothes bought for Michael were outgrown and replaced with bluer ones. His others had grown gray.

In the mornings I would play with his tummy because it was large, and fat and it made my heart beat a rapid, baby-smell-induced panic at the thought of leaving.... But of course, I would leave anyway. Robert was just around the corner.

When he came around the corner in the morning, he wore his towel because he showered after me. My work started earlier, or we allowed for my work to start earlier because his schedule was flexible.

As long as they're clean by Friday, he'd joke, and I of course would not get it because I had never read a book about window cleaners. To me, he had become the sort of thing we ridiculed when we moved to the city. A selection of phrases spoken in elevators or in moments between excel sheets.

I resisted this kind of talking.

His hand found its way around my waist, and I flinched. He retracted and I looked down and he sought my eyes, but I was like that, and so he frowned and then smiled and let me go and picked up Michael.

Michael started laughing and I watched my two men twirl around the kitchen giggling and making rah sounds. I smiled as I sipped my coffee, as I put on my coat... as I left.

"I'll see you tonight," I said, and he said I love you in the way that people do when they want to hear it back. The door was swinging. The door was closing, and I could not reach him in time.

On the corner, a policewoman blew her whistle and children crossed the street. All manner of people said hello to the lady because she was a policewoman dedicated to the children. This made her better than the other policemen and women, or it did, it seemed to the people on the block.

She nodded to me, and I nodded back, and I wondered what sort of relationship we shared as I turned and headed to the train. I thought about her as I climbed the steps and the baby fat, I had not yet shaken jiggled about my uterus.

Uteruses are sexy, I thought, but the train had already arrived. The mornings were better than the evenings. In the mornings I thought about getting on the train. On the train I read and off the train I walked. When I first started with Harper Collins, I got off blocks away from the office to strut around in my publishing clothes which are much like any sort of nice clothing, except with coffee stains and covered by sweaters that allowed the under-shirt's collar through the collar.

At a certain point the magic wore, and I got off the block the office shared with the station.

In the mornings, Samia would say hi and I would say hi back, but this morning she was not at her desk at the front of the office. Instead, she worked on the coffee machine to the rhythm of off-hand dialogue of one Mr. P.F. Goodrich. Mr. Goodrich wore a mustache in the way that the people in his corner of the office had taken to wearing mustaches. It was neither the style nor an irony of the style. Instead, they wore it for each other, but today, it seemed, he wore it for Samia who, despite her best efforts, continuously responded to the declarative inquiries to which she was obliged to respond.

"Old thing never works," he said. And she, Samia, then had to negotiate what exactly he wanted. Obviously, the statement was not a question, but it was very clearly her turn to speak. But there was nothing to latch onto, but this is the way with men. They show up and expect you to be interesting...

Or they don't. Some just expect you to be okay. To be happy, or not even happy, because of course they understand, no. Not happy, then. Just to be alive, content... present with them so that they might not feel alone. But of course, we're always alone.

I called to Samia and said there's a package for Mr. Collins, and Samia looked back gratefully and said, ah, I know just what for, and Mr. Goodrich waved, and I waved back and went to my desk. Samia went to hers and Mr. Goodrich did whatever it is men with mustaches liked to do in publishing houses. Robert didn't have a mustache. I laughed and told him I'd leave him if he decided to grow one, but that wasn't very funny and he took it somewhat personally, and so I apologized, and he said it didn't matter, but it did, and that is how we're here, avoiding eye contact in the kitchen.

At lunch, I went to Stan's which was a diner that served breakfast all day. Breakfast was always good, but I skipped it, and the concept of lunch revolted me and so I was a dinner-only sort of person. So were many in the city.

On my lunch breaks, I'd sit at Stan's, either indoors or out and publicly read or leaf through manuscripts as though I had thoughts that were bigger and brighter, and naturally more critical than the people sitting next to me. Privately, of course I thought they were, and from a third person's perspective, perhaps in some ways, what I had to say, or think was more considered than Mr. Goodrich, but this line of thinking has too many consequences, and so I kept it mostly to myself.

On Fridays, on occasion, for every Friday is too often, Harper-Collins hosted writer's parties where the newly published authors, that is to say authors releasing new books for the next quarter would sit around or walk around or stand outside on a patio on a floor several hundred feet above other the pavement and smoke and talk about themselves to people who were like them. And the publishing staff.

Here, of course, I could feel safe in saying that I thought I was smarter than the people around me, that my internal dialogue was of greater significance than they who found theirs printed, but of course someone smarter would say "to what end," and I would have to contemplate the time it takes to hit the ground from wherever we were standing.

On one such Friday I had determined that it would probably take a relatively long time, but success was guaranteed. A woman came up beside me and said it's beautiful isn't it. And I nodded and then she left, and a man replaced her and said the same thing and I looked at him and he lit a cigarette and I said, "Yeah," and found Samia.

Samia was my lifeline at Harper-Collins because everyone was either boring or an ass. At a certain point, when an office is filled with people who get along, you have to ask yourself whether or not you are the problem. *In my mind, this was not one of those occasions, but I was not without my problems, and so, at lunch, or on breaks, I would talk to Samia about my problems, and she would nod and tell me hers and she'd say things like, my therapist just talks to me about their problems, I think I'm going to leave her.*

I could never go to therapy, I'd say.

You should, you need it, she'd laugh.

And I'd say, yeah maybe,

And Samia would say that I was a better therapist than her real one and I wondered about what that meant.

These conversations were the day's pervading joy and at a certain point I became no better than Mr. Goodrich. Well, that's not quite true. My line of statements and questions were, at least, direct, and qualifiable, but my intentions were the same. Samia and I began staying later at lunch or after work and talking and wining and then dining and then Robert would call and I'd say I was with Samia reading a manuscript, which was often in the realm of truth. I would pretend that the last time was the last time, for who can predict the future?

Well, I could. And she could, and we did, often and sometimes twice in a day because for the love of Christ why not?

But the why-not is easily answered. Because Robert misses you, and you said you'd be there. Because Michael is an infant, and surely, he needs you for these years he won't remember. But how can life be like this? How can I already be so close to death? Married, trapped, en-mothered, and waiting... for what?

For what? I had screamed at Robert the night before. He blanched in fear, and I must have seemed like a crazy person, but that was okay because I knew that was how I must have seemed.

At least you are aware when you're acting unfairly, Samia had said, but after years of being aware of myself, I began to wonder whether I was doing it intentionally. And of course, the answer was yes and no, which never really helped anyone anyway.

Robert and I made love after he failed to console me. It was not his job to console me, he just failed at doing so. He failed at a lot of things, but that was not his fault. I often thought it was my fault because he always put my ambitions ahead of his own. This once felt supportive, but over time made me question his strength. It was not that I thought he lacked conviction so much as I felt like the embodiment of his direction.

Which is fine, for some people. Or I imagine that it is fine even if I disagree with the premise.

Today at the coffee shop I thought about it as I watched the couple exchange the ways they viewed themselves. I tell myself stories about this, one would say, and the other would say something equally prescribed, calculated, neurotic, affable, describable, and they would giggle or not giggle and instead nod to show the seriousness with which they listened to one another. But ask either to remember a word, I thought, and how many words would they remember?

But I was being shitty, and I knew I was being shitty and so I wondered why, and I supposed that I felt significantly worse today than I had expected. Nobody's fault, just the way it goes and so I left Stan's and wandered among the buildings. Robert paged me at 2:00 and Samia at 2:15.

But it was now 2:30. In the hour since Stan's I walked all the way to the bridge. At times, I'd look at the skyscrapers beside me searching for the sight of my husband. As though he could afford to spend time between squeegee strokes to pick his wife out of the throng. But maybe he did or would, I thought. He was the sort to think of doing so.

I watched the water lap at the boats that burbled along the river. If the fall didn't kill you, the water would, I'd remembered Robert saying. I did not like the sound of that: almost dying. Awful concept. Instead, I squinted up the cables that suspended the bridge and wondered if I could climb them. There was a path of sorts, guarded by an iron gate, but it was more prohibitive than preventative and so I thought about climbing them anyway.

Maybe at that height the water turns to asphalt.

My pager paged again. It was Michael's day-care. Robert never got around to picking him up from school. Where had the hours gone?

Mr. Goodrich's mustachioed master would be upset that I left work early, but now I had a reason. Throw it on my sick days, I'd say. To Robert, I ran that town.

I grabbed Michael from the day care, and he burbled like the boats as we practiced walking. Robert had not paged me back. He often had trouble reaching me after a particular windy day at work. On the hard days, he'd go to the bar with his window washing buddies and they all acted like men for a night.

"It's fun," he'd grin goofily. I came one time and found that it was mostly talking and throwing darts. It was weirdly vulnerable. Michael stumbled about the sidewalk.

The house was empty. I put Michael down and he burbled some gleeful reply before knocking amongst his blankets. The house was silent. So wonderfully, beautifully silent. Michael would not need food for another hour, and Robert, God love him, was wherever Roberts go. I collapsed into our armchair. Some lady said something in the street which elicited some reply from across the street. I listened for a while, letting their words wash over me.

The phone rang. I had almost nodded off. My back strained under the pressure of standing, but I answered.

"Yes, hello."

"Meredith?"

"Yes."

"You should probably sit down."

Marlot stopped reading. Zed, by this point, had elected to leg swinging and waiting for the story to end.

"It's different," she said. She meant different from her best seller.

"I know." Marlot shifted and bent and placed his laptop on the ground before standing, reaching into the sky, and groaning. He joined Zed on the lip. They watched their feet swing by one another. She passed over the bottle and they watched people laugh and go about whatever it is people do on Sunday nights.

He drank and passed the bottle back. She drank and she made a smacking sound with her mouth. The sugar dried on her tongue. He watched a trickle dribble from her lip and grinned as she wiped at it with her wrist.

She smiled, "What?"

He looked down. "I don't know."

A droplet dripped onto her forearm, and she looked into the sky. The city had all but disappeared behind the fog of clouds rolling from the far part of town. Even the moon, now, dipped behind the air. He made a shifted toward her and held her hand. The rain began to fall.

It all came faster now. The silence and the swinging, the rain drops, and the drinking carried their conversation from moms and dads to leaving and Marlot felt his eyes dampen at the thought.

How odd to feel so proud, he thought. Her face lit when she spoke of tomorrow. He scooted closer in the droplets, and she felt the water on her cheek as her head nodded to his shoulder. She shivered and he asked if she would like to go inside.

In a moment, she said, and then that moment came. Thunder clapped the sky and lightning shot amongst the buildings. The warm rush of rainfall blew their hair back from the edge and she made a squealing sound as they leapt from the edge of the building. A rush of dust plumed up the wall on which they were sitting as fatter drops, those from the meat of a storm, slapped on the rooftop.

She put her hands over hair and rushed to the door as Marlot lifted his laptop from the floor and slipped inside. His lanky body rushed down the pavement of the stairs and they stood among the water closets and mops, poorly hidden from the perpetual movements of building inhabitants, and listened to the storm collide with shingles.

A television played… a mother told her child something the child needed to hear. No, you can't trample around this apartment. Not in my house, she said, but Marlot was only listening in the way people do when they're watching a rocket lifting or when learning about the end of the world.

Their three hands became two and he held her. He quaked for a moment, and she quaked when she felt him shudder. He squeezed tighter and pulled apart: a slim space between them. So warm and yet escaping, resolving and in resolution, her; Jesus Christ, he thought.

Jesus Christ, she thought, his tears were wet against her cheeks.

*

Once more it was morning. The light that ripped, took pause and, in this morning, gave the pair a moment. She pushed him back inside her and their breath, heavy with tobacco, sex, and wine, tasted like them if not also salty. He kissed her chest and threaded his fingers behind the nape of her neck. They did not come together, but separate, in time, and they passed on into dawn.

Here is the girl, she is dressing. Here is the boy, he is dressing. Here is the bus, it is moving. This is her house, she is leaving. This is her house, they are leaving. This is the train, it is waiting, and he is waiting, and she is waiting.

"I don't know what I would have done without you," he wants to say. He wants to say, "I love you," but it's not the right thing to say.

Instead, he makes a sound and smiles and pulls her in and says, "Be safe," and she says, "I love you too," but now the doors are closing.

The END

Our Authors

A Medic's Mind by Matthew Heneghan

Dreams Of You by Jeremiah Valentine

Order Of Zendarkin by John Patrick

Spiritual Lessons Learned From A Year Of Struggle: Teaching during COVID-19 by Traci Musick Shaffer

Ravenswood Hall by E Atkinson (Book 1 of The Grace Beale Series)

Ticket To Botany Bay by E Atkinson (Book 2 of The Grace Beale Series)

At The Going Down Of The Sun by E Atkinson (Book 3 of The Grace Beale Series)